NANDI AND NZURI
AND
THE ANCIENT STONES

BY KAREN MABHENA

ONCE UPON A TIME, IN THE BEAUTIFUL VAST LAND OF AFRICA
LIVED TWO BEAUTIFUL GIRLS NAMED NANDI AND NZURI.
NANDI AND NZURI WERE BEST FRIENDS AND LOVED GOING ON
ADVENTURES TOGETHER TO DISCOVER DIFFERENT MYSTERIOUS
PARTS OF THE AFRICAN CONTINENT.

"MUMMY, DADDY, CAN WE PLEASE GO FOR TODAY'S ADVENTURE? WE PROMISE WE WON'T GO FAR," ASKS NANDI. "WE WILL BE BACK BEFORE THE SUN SETS," INSISTS NZURI. "OF COURSE, YOU MAY. MAKE SURE YOU TELL US ALL ABOUT IT WHEN YOU RETURN," SAYS NANDI'S DAD. "DON'T MISS SUPPER," LAUGHS NZURI'S MUM.

THE GIRLS SET OFF ON THEIR ADVENTURE AS THE SUN SHOWED THEM THE WAY. THEY PASSED BY THEIR FRIENDLY NEIGHBOURS, WHO ALWAYS MADE SURE THE GIRLS PASSED SAFELY. "HELLO MR. AND MRS. LEKOTA," SAID THE GIRLS TO THEIR NEIGHBOR'S. "HELLO, NANDI AND NZURI. MAKE SURE YOU FOLLOW THE PATH THE SUN HAS SET FOR YOU," SAID MR. AND MRS. LEKOTA. "WE WILL," SAID THE GIRLS AS THEY SKIPPED TO THEIR ADVENTURE

THEN THE SUN SHINED EVEN BRIGHTER. THIS WAS A SIGN
THAT THEY HAVE ARRIVED AT THEIR NEXT ADVENTURE.
THE GIRLS HAD STUMBLED ACROSS SOME OLD STONE
RUINS. THE GIRLS WALKED AROUND THE MYSTERIOUS
STONE RUINS, WONDERING WHAT THEY ARE. PUZZLED
AS TO WHAT THEY WERE SEEING, THE GIRLS CLOSED
THEIR EYES AND ASKED THE SUN TO SHOW THEM THE
MAGIC. THEN THE GIRLS WERE WHISKED AWAY INTO A
VORTEX OF IMAGINATION LANE.

THE GIRLS ARRIVED AT A FASCINATING PLACE, JUST LIKE THE STONE RUINS THEY HAD JUST STUMBLED ACROSS. "NZURI, WHERE ARE WE?" ASKED NANDI LOOKING SO PUZZLED. "I DON'T KNOW NANDI, BUT IT SEEMS LIKE A MAGICAL PLACE," REPLIED NZURI. THE GIRLS, FASCINATED, WALKED AROUND THE PLACE, WONDERING WHERE THEY WERE.

A YOUNG BOY APPROACHED NANDI AND NZURI AND
NOTICED THAT THEY SEEMED LOST. "I DON'T THINK
I HAVE SEEN YOU BEFORE. ARE YOU LOOKING FOR
SOMEONE?" ASKED THE BOY. "WE ARE NOT QUITE
FROM HERE," SAYS NZURI. WE COME FROM A PLACE
NOT TOO FAR FROM HERE, JUST FOR ASHORT VISIT.
"OH, WELCOME TO THE BEAUTIFUL LAND OF MZANSI.

MY NAME IS NAMIBO" SAID THE BOY. "HI NAMIBO, MY NAME IS NZURI" "AND I'M NANDI." NAMIBO TAKES THE GIRLS AROUND THE AREA TO SHOW THEM HOW BEAUTIFUL IT IS. THE PLACE WHERE I FOUND YOU IS CALLED "INZALO YE LANGA" IT MEANS THE BIRTHPLACE OF THE SUN. IT IS A CALENDAR WE USE THAT TELLS US WHAT SEASON WE ARE IN DURING THE YEAR AND MUCH MORE!

EVERYONE THERE IN THE COMMUNITY IS VERY FRIENDLY AND WELCOMING. THEY ALL GREET THE GIRLS AND WELCOME THEM. THE GIRLS CHEERFULLY GREET BACK, FEELING VERY EXCITED AT WHAT THEY ARE SEEING. NAMIBO TAKES THE GIRLS TO PLAY WITH OTHER CHILDREN. "MUSA AND TSEPISO," SHOUTED NAMIBO, "COME AND MEET SOME NEW FRIENDS TO PLAY WITH." MUSA AND TSEPISO WERE SOME OF THE CHILDREN OF MZANSI . THEY WERE VERY FRIENDLY. "COME, THESE ARE NEW FRIENDS," SAID MUSA. "WE ARE PLAYING DODGEBALL TODAY," SAYS TSEPISO.

THE GIRLS PLAYED AND PLAYED WITH OTHER CHILDREN
WHEN TWO VERY IMPORTANT PEOPLE CAME TO MEET
THEM. "LOOKS LIKE WE HAVE SOME VISITORS TODAY.
HELLO THERE! ARE YOU HAVING FUN?" ASKS THE MAN.
SURPRISED, NANDI REPLIES, "YES, WE ARE HAVING LOTS
OF FUN. EVERYONE HERE IS SO KIND TO US. MY NAME
IS NANDI AND THIS IS MY BEST FRIEND NZURI"
"HELLO OUR DEAR VISITORS, MY NAME IS QUEEN
AYANDA AND THIS IS MY HUSBAND, KING JABU."
"WELCOME TO THE BEAUTIFUL LAND OF MZANSI,"
SAYS THE KING.

THE KING AND QUEEN TALK TO THE GIRLS ABOUT MZANSI. "WE LIVE IN A PEACEFUL COMMUNITY WHERE EVERYONE WORKS TOGETHER AND SHARES EVERYTHING. WE GROW FOOD TOGETHER, BUILD TOGETHER AND EVEN CELEBRATE TOGETHER. WE CALL THIS "UBUNTU," SAYS THE QUEEN. THEN THE KING ALSO ADDS," UBUNTU IS OUR WAY OF LIFE HERE AND IT MEANS WE ARE ALL ONE PEOPLE. THAT'S HOW WE WERE ABLE TO BUILD THIS COMMUNITY." NANDI AND NZURI WERE SO FASCINATED BY WHAT THEY WERE LEARNING AND SEEING. THERE WAS LOTS OF FOOD, BEAUTIFUL HOMES, HAPPY PEOPLE, ADVANCED TECHNOLOGY. EVERYTHING IS GOOD HERE. THE GIRLS ENJOYED SO MUCH THAT THEY ALMOST FORGOT IT WAS ALMOST TIME TO GO HOME.

"LOOK NZURI, THE SUN IS ABOUT TO SET; THAT MEANS IT'S TIME FOR US TO GO BACK HOME," SAYS NANDI. "I'M AFRAID WE HAVE TO GO NOW, KING JABU AND QUEEN AYANDA. WE REALLY ENJOYED OUR TIME HERE, " SAYS NZURI. "IT WAS A PLEASURE HAVING YOU HERE GIRLS" SAYS THE KING. SOME MEMBERS OF THE COMMUNITY, THE KING AND QUEEN ESCORT THE GIRLS. AS THEY SAID THEIR GOODBYES AND WAVED TO ONE ANOTHER, THE GIRLS WENT BACK INTO THE VORTEX AND BACK HOME AT THE OLD STONE STRUCTURE

"THAT WAS SO FUN NANDI, I CAN'T WAIT FOR US TO TELL EVERYONE WHAT HAPPENED TONIGHT AT THE FIRE AFTER SUPPER," SAYS NZURI. "YAY, LET'S GO HOME AND TELL EVERYBODY!" SAYS NANDI

THE GIRLS FOLLOW THE SUN'S TRAIL BACK HOME; THEY PASS BY MR. AND MRS. LEKOTA, WHO WERE HAPPY TO SEE THE GIRLS MAKING THEIR WAY BACK HOME SAFELY TILL THEY ARRIVED HOME EXCITED TO TELL EVERYONE WHAT HAPPENED.

AFTER SUPPER, ALL THE PEOPLE AROUND THE COMMUNITY GATHERED TO HEAR ABOUT NANDI AND NZURI'S GREAT ADVENTURE. NANDI AND NZURI SHARED EACH AND EVERY DETAIL OF THEIR STORY TO THE WHOLE COMMUNITY AND EVERYONE WAS FASCINATED BY THE STORY OF THE GIRL'S ADVENTURE.

THE STORY WAS SO AMAZING THAT AFTERWARDS, EVERYONE DANCED AND SANG AROUND THE FIRE IN JOY AND CELEBRATION UNDER THE BEAUTIFUL AFRICAN SKIES

THIS BOOK IS ESPECIALLY DEDICATED TO ALL CHILDREN OF AFRICAN DESCENT. MAY YOUR LIGHT SHINE BRIGHT AS TOMORROW'S LEADERS!

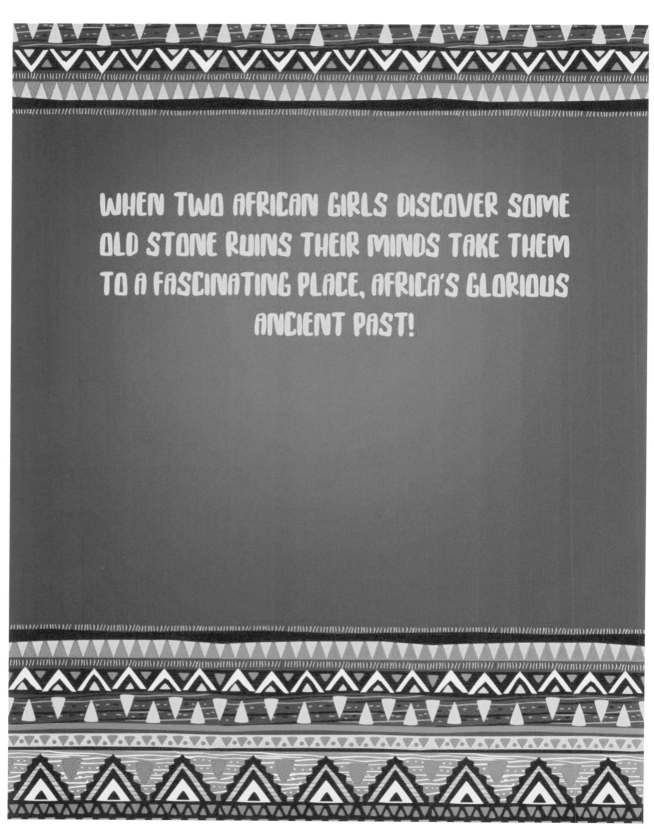

WHEN TWO AFRICAN GIRLS DISCOVER SOME OLD STONE RUINS THEIR MINDS TAKE THEM TO A FASCINATING PLACE, AFRICA'S GLORIOUS ANCIENT PAST!